Looking Out for Sarah

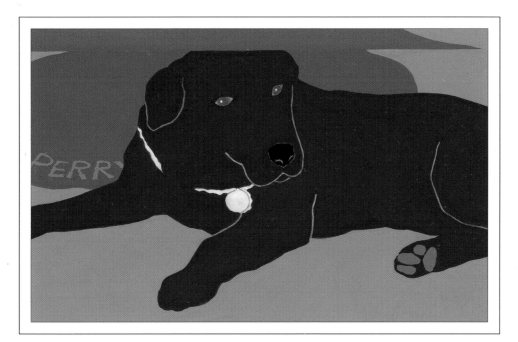

Written and Illustrated by
Glenna Lang

ini Charlesbridge

To
Pat and Saxon
Gloria and Mack
Tina and Carmen
and all the other Sarah and Perry teams everywhere…

With many thanks to the people at Guiding Eyes for the Blind
for all their encouragement and support. Special thanks to
Kim Charlson, librarian at the Perkins School for the Blind,
for helping me research this subject. And with much love and
gratitude to Sarah and Perry for their patience, friendship,
and for helping me to explore new terrain.

In the early morning light, Perry felt Sarah stirring above him. He raised his sleepy eyelids, looked out from his pillow, and waited eagerly for her feet to touch the floor.

A wag filled Perry's tail and traveled up his back. His paws landed in her lap.
He licked Sarah's chin as she spoke to him in sweet tones.

GUIDE DOG LEADS BLIND PERSON
FROM BOSTON TO NEW YORK

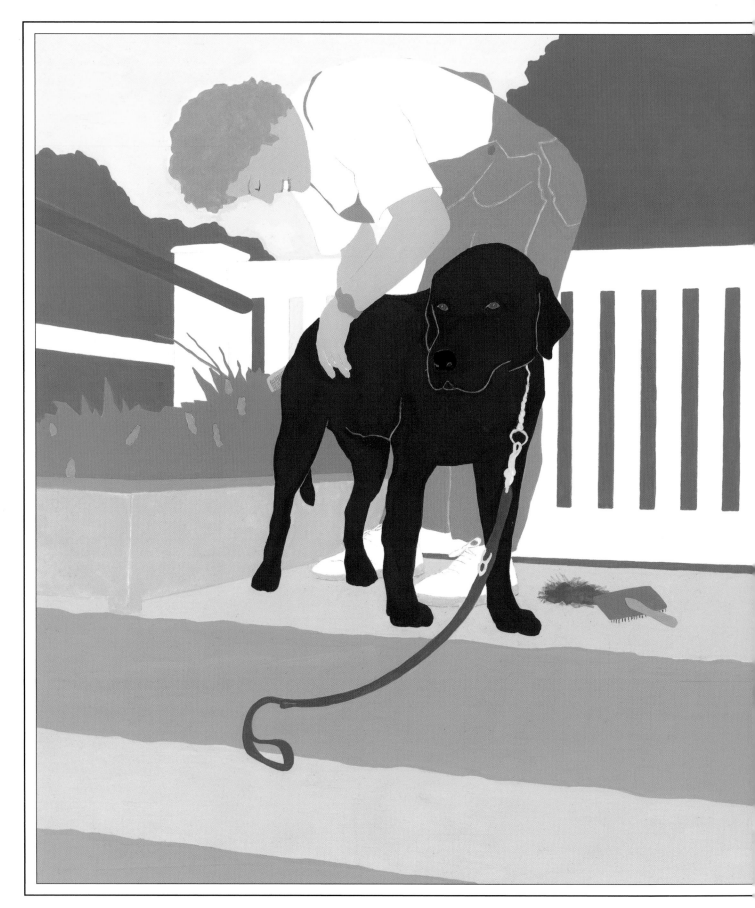

After breakfast, Sarah brushed the itches out of Perry's short thick coat. He squinted happily when she groomed that place on his back that he never could reach.

Perry loved their walks. He held still while Sarah buckled his harness around him. When his harness was on, he was working and had to listen carefully for directions. Where would he lead Sarah today?

"Left, Perry," said Sarah. As they strode down the sidewalk, Perry pulled to the side to sniff a tasty crumb. He knew he shouldn't eat on the job, but he hoped Sarah wouldn't mind just once. "Hup up, Perry," Sarah corrected him. Perry snapped back to his work.

At the corner Perry stopped and waited for Sarah's instructions. "Forward, Perry." He checked to make sure no traffic was coming. Although Sarah knew when he was eyeing a bagel, she needed help not bumping into things and avoiding cars.

When they got to their favorite grocery store, Perry paused to see if Sarah wanted to go inside. "OK, Perry." They walked through the automatic doors into the narrow aisles.

Perry was hot. He lay down on the cool linoleum floor and enjoyed the smell from the bakery trays. He was the only dog in most stores. Sometimes he saw other dogs tied outside, waiting for their people, but he and Sarah were always together.

At the post office, Perry waited for Sarah to find the bottom step with her foot. Then he climbed slowly so that Sarah could step up when she felt his harness rise. "Good boy, Perry," she thanked him. His tail wagged gently whenever Sarah praised him.

After their errands, they returned to their front gate. Perry looked hopefully for Sarah's "O.K." Inside their house, Perry lapped cool water from his bowl. He curled up on the braided rug for a rest before going back to work.

Refreshed from his nap, Perry carefully wove their way through the crowd at the train station and allowed extra room for Sarah's guitar. He saw a crumb but kept on going. Finding a path through the moving people required all his concentration.

Perry liked the rocking motion of the train. He tried to get some of himself under the seat so that people wouldn't step on him. When the train stopped, he had to maneuver Sarah around duffel bags and across the gap between the train and the platform.

The train, the guitar, the purple sweater…. Perry suspected they were going to one of the schools they often visited. He followed Sarah's directions all the way there and into a large sunny room. He wagged when he saw the children's faces at the same height as his. Their hands smelled like peanut butter and jelly, or tunafish.

Perry lay back quietly while Sarah sang and strummed. Soon she had everyone singing and swaying and smiling. She even sang a song about Perry. He pricked up his ears when he heard his name.

Afterwards Perry guided Sarah to a classroom. The children asked Sarah many questions. She told them that Perry was seven years old. He was trained at a guide dog school. Yes, she and Perry once walked from Boston to New York to show the world what a guide dog can do for a blind person. It was a great adventure.

Sarah passed around photos of their walk and said it was O.K. to pat Perry now.
But when Perry or another guide dog was working, they shouldn't pat or distract him.
Being patted was Perry's favorite part of school. He snuggled against several laps
and enjoyed the gentle hands stroking his fur. He slipped into a dreamy sleep…

Perry dreamt about the time he and Sarah walked all day every day for a month along country paths and small town sidewalks. He had to keep a constant lookout for tree roots, potholes, and the ditches alongside dirt roads. He made sure to look up high so that Sarah would not hit her head on branches.

Each night they slept at someone's house or at a motel. Perry savored the smell of mole holes, plush carpet, and greasy diners. His muscles grew strong and his pads grew tough. Crowds of people came to cheer them on.

Television cameras whirred softly. Photographers snapped their fingers at Perry to make him look up. Reporters interviewed them—although Perry was not much of a publicity hound. They walked on and on.

Together they met and walked with many people, even mayors of cities.
The mayors made speeches and complimented Perry. When they reached New York
City, he and Sarah each received a large shiny tag. His chest swelled with pride....
Perry woke up with a smile.

After their school visit, Perry and Sarah joined a friend at a restaurant with wooden booths and soft carpet. Perry's eyes widened when he saw all the crumbs under the table. He quietly took care of them while glancing up at Sarah. Luckily she did not notice. The waiter brought him a large bowl of water.

Perry always looked forward to his daily play session. He found the shortcut, a hole in the fence around the park, and carefully led Sarah in. The smell of the tennis ball made his tail swing wildly. Sarah removed his harness.

Perry never grew tired of bringing the ball back to Sarah. Each throw was as exciting as the last. He bounded over small bushes and flowers, and sped through the grass with his thundering paws.

He loved the feel of the wind flattening his ears. But when Sarah called, "Perry, come!" his tail drooped, his head sagged, and his run turned into a reluctant walk as he returned for his harness. He panted all the way home.

After his dinner, Perry lay down near Sarah at the piano bench. The breeze wafted in. Her piano notes filled the air. Her singing tingled his ears. The sounds rang round and mellow.

Sometimes the light of the moon or the sound of fire engines could move Perry the same way. An uncontrollable howl rose in his throat. He jumped up and sang one last joyous song with Sarah before heading up to bed.

When Sarah pulled up her covers, Perry slithered onto his pillow. The cedar chips inside it smelled like the playground at school today. Sarah's shoes still had a faint aroma of train station, dinner rolls, and grass. He settled his nose on his paws and heaved a contented sigh. It had been a long day looking out for Sarah.

About the Characters

This book is based on a real black Labrador retriever named Perry and his owner, Sarah Gregory Smith.

Perry was born on a farm and was carefully chosen as a potential guide dog. He was placed with a family who adored him and taught him basic obedience such as "sit" and "lie down." When he was fourteen months old, because he was an eager learner and had such a pleasing disposition, he left to attend a guide dog school run by Guiding Eyes for the Blind in Yorktown Heights, New York. There he worked hard with his trainer for six months.

At the guide dog school, Sarah met Perry for the first time. They spent time getting to know each other, and the trainer taught Sarah the commands that Perry knew. Many people attended Perry's graduation ceremony, including Perry's first family who were very proud of him. Afterwards, Sarah and Perry went back to Sarah's home in Salem, Massachusetts.

Since losing her sight as an adult from a disease called diabetes, Sarah has continued to teach dance and music. Besides being active in her community's soup kitchen (where she is a cook), politics, and her church, she also is a square- and contra-dance-caller and performs in folk concerts for adults and children, often with her musician-husband, Bill Smith. Perry always accompanies them.

Together Perry and Sarah enjoy many activities, including swimming, sailing, and camping. And they really did walk three hundred miles from Boston to New York when Perry was six years old.

Published by Charlesbridge
85 Main Street
Watertown, MA 02472
(617) 926-0329
www.charlesbridge.com

Library of Congress Cataloging-in-Publication Data
Lang, Glenna.
Looking Out for Sarah / Glenna Lang.
p. cm.
Summary: Describes a day in the life of a seeing eye dog,
from going with his owner to the grocery store and post office,
to visiting a class of school children, and playing ball.
Also describes their three-hundred-mile walk from Boston to New York.
ISBN-13: 978-0-88106-647-0; ISBN-10: 0-88106-647-8 (reinforced for library use)
ISBN-13: 978-1-57091-607-6; ISBN-10: 1-57091-607-1 (softcover)
[1. Guide dogs—Fiction. 2. Dogs—Fiction. 3. Blind—Fiction.] I. Title.

PZ7.L2525 Lo2001
[Fic]—dc21   00-037714

Printed in Korea
(hc) 10 9 8 7 6 5 4 3
(sc) 10 9 8 7 6 5

Illustrations painted in gouache on Arches watercolor paper
Display type and text type set in Adobe Palatino
Color separations by South China Printing Company, Hong Kong
Printed and bound February 2010 by Sung In Printing in Gunpo-Si, Kyonggi-Do, Korea
Production supervision by Brian G. Walker
Designed by Glenna Lang